W9-BKR-245

AMAZONA

Dedicated to those who have had to flee, leaving their lives behind
May the light in their hearts never fade

May it light new paths
So its brightness can blind the greedy

ACCIÓN CULTURAL
ESPAÑOLA

This book was supported by a grant from Acción Cultural Española (AC/E)

Story and art by Canizales
English-language translation by Sofía Huitrón Martínez

First American edition published in 2022 by Graphic Universe™

The author will be donating a proportion of his royalties for this book to Resguardo Indígena Nasa de Cerro Tijeras

Graphic Universe™
An imprint of Lerner Publishing Group, Inc.
241 First Avenue North
Minneapolis, MN 55401 USA

For reading levels and more information, look up this title at www.lernerbooks.com.

Main body text set in Dinkle.
Typeface provided by Chank.

Library of Congress Cataloging-in-Publication Data

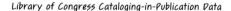

Names: Canizales, author, illustrator. | Huitrón Martínez, Sofía, translator.
Title: Amazona / Canizales ; translated by Sofia Huitron Martinez.
Description: First American edition. | Minneapolis, MN : Graphic Universe, 2022. | Audience: Ages 14–18 | Audience: Grades 10–12 | Summary: "Andrea, a young Indigenous Colombian woman, has returned to the land she calls home. She comes to mourn her child—and to capture evidence of the illegal mining that displaced her family" —Provided by publisher.
Identifiers: LCCN 2021027632 (print) | LCCN 2021027633 (ebook) | ISBN 9781728401706 (library binding) | ISBN 9781728448671 (paperback) | ISBN 9781728444093 (ebook)
Subjects: CYAC: Graphic novels. | Indigenous peoples—Colombia—Fiction. | Family life—Colombia—Fiction. | Gold mines and mining—Fiction. | Colombia—Fiction. | LCGFT: Graphic novels.
Classification: LCC PZ7.7.C3634 Am 2022 (print) | LCC PZ7.7.C3634 (ebook) | DDC 741.5/9861—dc23

LC record available at https://lccn.loc.gov/2021027632
LC ebook record available at https://lccn.loc.gov/2021027633

Manufactured in the United States of America
1-48222-48809-11/2/2021

AMAZONA

CANIZALES

TRANSLATED FROM SPANISH BY SOFÍA HUITRÓN MARTÍNEZ

Graphic Universe™ • Minneapolis

No, I'm not a white woman.
No, I'm not half-clothed in pieces of a flag.
No, I don't care about looking sexy while
trying to save my world.

But yes, I am a woman of the Amazon, and I have returned to settle some issues.

The last time I was here, I was running from the bullets of people in fatigues.

They are still here, a few yards away, surrounding our sacred land and ready to spit fire at me the moment they see me.

We no longer live in the Amazonia region. We were displaced eleven months ago.
Now we are forced to live in the city of Cali, Colombia.

An organization decided it was better to keep us hidden in a dilapidated house in the city center
than have us out in the streets, where we would tarnish the city's festive landscape.

"How ungrateful!"
you might say. But let me ask:
How many people live in your house?

In the place where we live now, and forgive me if I don't call it home, you'll find: my sisters and brothers . . .

My cousins and aunts and uncles . . .

My neighbors, grandmothers, and grandfathers . . .

And boys and girls who lost their own families. A total of thirty-eight people sharing a 600-square-foot space. The place is divided into two rooms with no windows, a bathroom with no door, a kitchen, and a patio.

The local system of commerce is not for us. Money is not a great part of our culture. Yet without it, something seems to be missing.

Things are different here. You either look down and see trash on the ground or look up and see eyes that avoid your own.

Andrea, guess what? The other day, a lady gave me a slice of bread.

We don't beg like that, Lily! We aren't beggars. We're people whose land has been taken from us.

We find our own solutions. We don't wait for others to "save" us.

But everything here costs money!

Not everything, guys.

Along with the mangos, which the children ate so happily and which we could share with everybody, the tree gave me a secret:

Don't stay put. Move! You can do something!

Would we be able to go back? The question ate away at my soul.

Memories of the trees, the reeds, the frogs, the monkeys, the flowers, the water . . .
became things I could only see in my dreams.

My laughter had echoed throughout our old home, past my father, my mother, my husband, Julian, Esmeralda,
and Esteban. Now the only thing in that house is what the bullets have written across it: desolation.

A few weeks after we were forced to leave, my brother Julian dared to go back to our village, without telling anyone. But he could not get in.

He told us the place was unrecognizable. The ancient trees had been chopped down. A wire fence surrounded everything, impossible to cross.

He didn't dare leave his hiding spot between the bushes. Only a few steps away stood outposts with armed guards inside. Their expressions left no doubt that they would shoot at anyone who came close.

Back then, we weren't as far away from our village as we are now.

Cali

Starting back, I traveled twelve hours on a coach bus from Cali to Pitalito.

Colombia

Cali

Pitalito
Puerto Asís
my village

After that, I continued for another eight hours on a run-down chiva to Puerto Asís.

Amazonia Region

Pitalito

Puerto Asís

From there, the road becomes nothing but mud and rocks. But a few vans, gualas, run twice a day. I had to wait three hours for the next van, and after a two-hour ride, I was dropped off at a port on the Putumayo River.

my village

Putumayo River

At the port, I convinced a boatman, carrying exotic fruit for sale, to take me to a bend in the river . . .

Amazon River

... The point from which I've been walking for the last four hours, without a map or a compass.

And here I am, feeling the energy of the earth once again. It is wonderful, after almost a year.

The jaguar is the one
that guided me here.

A few days ago, in a
vision, it told me I had to
come back and reclaim
what is ours.

"How?" I said.
"That's impossible!"

It replied:

"I am the voice within you. At every
moment, you will know what you
must do, where you must go."

This is as far as my brother got.

A few more steps and I'll be fully visible
to those vicious armed guards.

The jaguar pushes me to keep going. I don't know if it's
playing a trick on me, but it keeps telling me something
I still don't believe to be true:

DO NOT ENTER

PAS[SE]RS WILL BE SHOT

"You are more powerful
than their bullets."

*Dialogue within brackets is spoken in the Spanish language. Dialogue is otherwise spoken in the local dialect of the Quechua language.

<Tell me, Amazona. You ever tried listening to the radio in the jungle?>

<Our heroes are ready for the confrontation ahead . . .>

<Ever spend hour after hour moving from one damn place to another to see if you can hear anything?>

<The fans can't wait, doing the wave from one side of the stadium to the other . . .>

<You haven't, right? Now, if I sit right here . . .

Crossing my leg and holding the radio like this . . .

I can get a clear signal and listen to the game.>

<The tension is rising, ladies and gentlemen! The match is about to begin!>

<But I'm sure you don't give a damn about that . . .

Let's see . . .

The commercials are starting . . . You've got one minute to tell me . . .

<Stay tuned and don't touch that dial, everybody. We'll be back in a few minutes for the start of the game!>

Why the hell have you decided to ruin my Colombia-Uruguay match?>

Good morning.

<Good lord! So, you don't even speak my language!

Maybe I'd better let something else do the talking . . . >

<This!>

BANG

That's why I'm asking you. Please, let me in. It will only take a minute! I'll bury my offering in the land, and I'll be gone. I've traveled all the way from Cali. It's a three-day trip! I came just for this . . .

Whew.

You're putting me in a tough spot . . .

What if you want to plant a bomb?

What do you have in that box?

My daughter.

<Hey, Cholo. Why is she still here?

What are you two talking about?!>

<Look, Salfumán, this is a very . . . unique situation. Turns out this girl used to live in the area. Remember the abandoned huts at the end of the mine? Well, that was her tribe. She's been traveling for three days, and all she wants is a moment to go and bury her daughter.>

My daughter's chance to join our ancestors depended on the decision of these men.

Those seconds when I could only watch their body language felt like years to me.

Something made me turn toward the jungle, and then . . . I saw it!

The jaguar was with me!

Sorry, Andrea. That was the only way Salfumán would let you in. He trusts no one.

<Only thirty minutes, Cholo. **That's it!**>

The remaining huts are up the hill, past the mine.

Thank you for helping me, Cholo.

Aah!
Oh, no . . .

This . . . this place used to be full of life. Full of trees and animals! . . . This is a **crime!**

I felt as if the harm had been done to me . . . as if parts of my life had been stripped away.

Let's go . . .
We have farther to walk.
There's not much time,
Andrea.

It's because of the game!
They let everyone leave
three hours early.

Why does the area seem like it's abandoned? No one's working.

There was a drawing to see who would stay and keep guard. As you can probably tell, Salfumán and I had to stay.

Wow! Soccer must be the most important thing in the world around here!

Well, this game **is** crucial. We'll find out if Colombia can make it to the World Cup quarterfinals!

Crucial? Can a soccer game save someone's life?

I don't know if . . .

Hey, was one of these . . .

. . . your house?

Click

Click

Click

You almost ready?

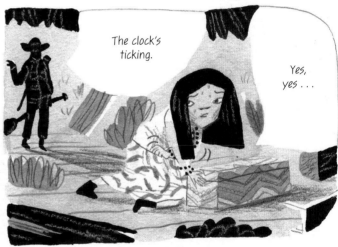

The clock's ticking.

Yes, yes . . .

Where do you want . . . uhh . . . your daughter to rest?

Where our ancestors sleep . . .

It's up here.

From this point on, the land is sacred. Please don't follow me!

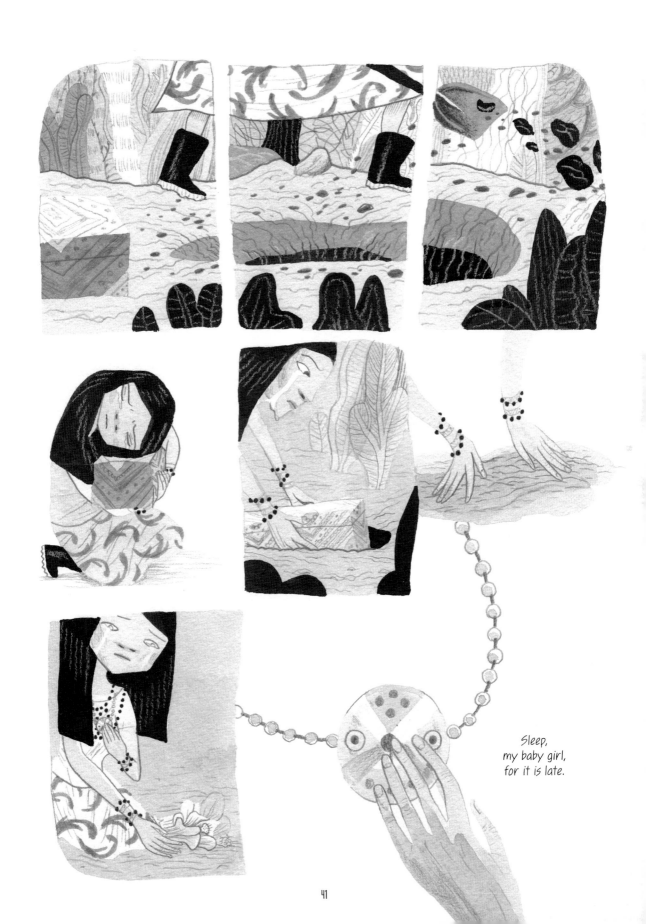

Sleep,
my baby girl,
for it is late.

Click Click Click

46

Still a couple of minutes left.

I can sit for a bit . . .

Ow! Damn!

Got so many things in my wallet that my butt hurts when I sit down.

All right, Cholo. Time to toss out some trash.

Mostly old receipts. Don't even know why I held onto all of these . . .

Oh!

After Six Months without "Don Fermín," a Son's Search Continues

Fermin Casarabe Nimijoy
missing fruit and vegetable vendor

The beloved owner of "Don Fermín's Fruits and Vegetables," Fermin Casarabe Nimijoy, has been missing for six months. His 14-year-old son, Elkin Casarabe, who is now running the family business, said the following:

"He was being accused by some men in uniform of being a guerilla collaborator. My father sold produce to anyone who would buy. Those men wanted my father to reveal where the guerilla fighters were hiding. As if he had a clue! A month after the incident, he didn't come home at night. I'm sure it was those men who took him. I am asking the authorities to please help me find where my father is."

State authorities have declined to comment.

What did they do with you, Dad?

48

So who's it looking at now? You or me?

I think it's looking at both of us!

Look, Elkin! It likes this necklace!

That one's my favorite too.

Does your father make them?

Yeah.

I can only give you this, Andrés. I'm sorry . . . your necklaces barely sell anymore.

Fermín, please! That's **half** of what you gave me last time!

Wait, I have some coins in my pocket . . . Let me see.

How about now? Better?

Andrea, let's go.

Huh? Okay, Papa.

59

Papa,
I'm so sorry.

What are you
talking about,
sweetie?

I'm very proud
of you!

‹Yeah . . .

Everything's
going
smoothly.

We're on our
way back now.
Over and out.›

Unbelievable!

So it's
you . . .

You're
that . . .

. . . Andrea.

I took advantage of your goodwill.

You didn't turn me in . . . despite all the shame that caused you and your father . . .

I never thanked you.

Instead, you almost killed me twice.

Twice?

You weren't part of that group a year ago? The one that shot at us in the middle of the night and kicked us off our land?

My husband and I saw men in fatigues heading toward our village.

He ran in the other direction
to divert them . . .

I ran to warn
everyone.

We went up the
mountain to our
sacred land, where
the jungle is thicker.

I came back because
I wanted to know
what had happened
to my husband.

BANG!

\<The huts are over here! That bastard was distracting us!\>

\<Listen up! Everyone! Come out of your houses now!\>

BANG BANG RATA TATA TATA TATA

Mama Leonor, the jaguar just showed us a path!

Then it has spoken to all of us through you.

Quick! Let's go to where Andrea is pointing. And be quiet!

You weren't able to find us.

We walked the whole night without taking a break. No one spoke. We moved forward without stopping.

When the sun came out, we were still deep in the rain forest.

Finally, we reached a nearby village with lots of pretty doors . . . which happened to be shut.

We tried to talk to the people, but the only ones who answered were the dogs.

Exhausted, we spent the next night in a soccer field . . . In the dark, it looked as if the field was full of dead bodies.

The next day, we arrived in Puerto Asís, where we found medical attention and food . . . The local hospital got in contact with an organization in Cali that said it could help us.

For two days, we zigzagged along a highway that made everyone sick.

When we arrived in Cali, it turned out that another Indigenous community—from Cauca, also displaced—had already taken the spots reserved for us. Instead, we were put up in temporary tents on a public park.

Local authorities relocated us to the outskirts of town while they prepared an empty house for us . . .

The house is in an area with a lot of crime. It's not safe, so we have to take turns guarding the place. It's not hospitable at all . . . But we make do in the few square feet we have. Still—we can't stay there. At night, it's hard to breathe. There's no good airflow, and there are too many of us. My daughter died from a lack of oxygen.

One night, a friend's cousin came by and told me he knew a guy who knew something about my papa.

Sabogal knows who killed him.

Sabogal? From the jungle? I'd . . . rather stay away from those people.

You're going to let your father's disappearance go unpunished?

I'll come get you at six.

He did . . . and we went to the outskirts of town.

And in the middle of the jungle was Sabogal.

I was sweating . . . If the wrong people see you with someone, they immediately associate you with them.

He gave me very vague information. He only said how I would make more money working for them and that they would help me find my father and see justice done . . .

And that they would be like a family to me.

Click

Click

Click

It's hard to explain . . . but I felt as if I was flying . . .
As if the jungle opened up as I went . . .
Perhaps it was the overpowering excitement of the hope of getting our land back . . .
Of knowing that I carried with me the evidence we needed to reopen the case . . .

I love it, Papa!
It's so, so beautiful!

I knew you'd like it.

Here, I'll help you put
it on, sweetie.

Whenever you can, bring it with you and wear it close to your heart . . .

I'll never want to take it off!

. . . Because it represents the jaguar. Its wisdom, its power. If you have it with you, it will show you the way.

And when everything gets so complicated that you feel there's no way out . . .

You know what it will do for you?

What?

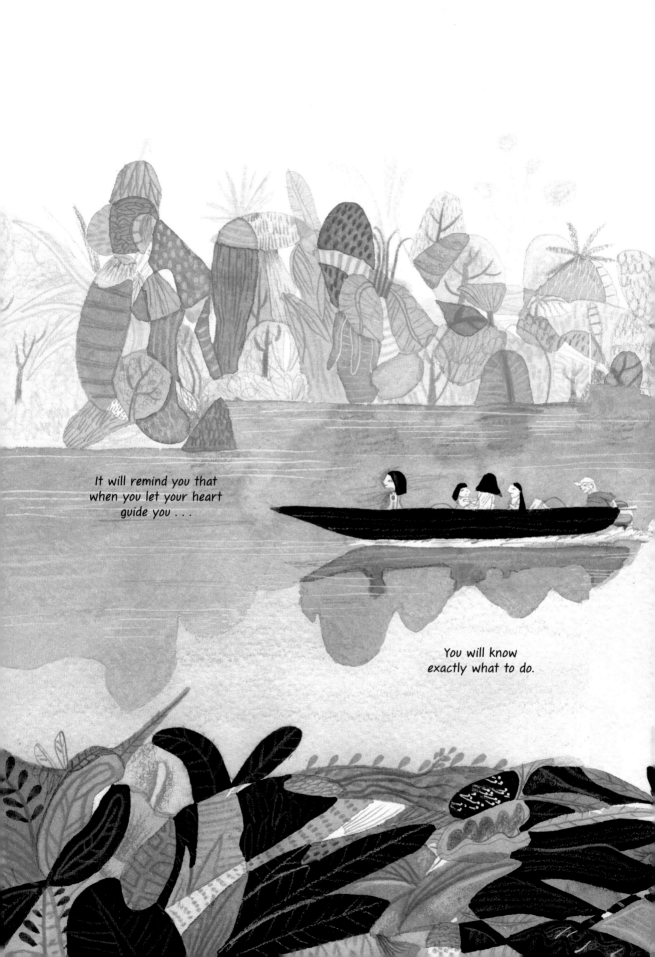

It will remind you that
when you let your heart
guide you . . .

You will know
exactly what to do.

Because in that
moment . . .

The jaguar is you!

AFTER *AMAZONA*

Although Andrea is a fictional creation, the story of *Amazona* has been inspired by real conditions affecting the many Indigenous peoples of Colombia. In the years since 2014, when the story takes place, and since 2018 to 2019, when Canizales created this graphic novel, a combination of forces has continued to threaten, displace, and disappear people from Indigenous groups across the country. According to the International Work Group for Indigenous Affairs, the Indigenous population of Colombia includes approximately 1,500,000 individuals; the country's 2018 census places that number at more than 1,900,000 individuals from 115 different native peoples. In a country of more than 50 million people, they are disproportionately harmed by acts of violence and corruption.

Alongside the country's Afro-Colombian peoples, Indigenous Colombians face forced displacement, and efforts to resist are fraught. A variety of organizations consider Colombia the most dangerous nation in the world for human-rights defenders. As of 2019, Colombia's human-rights ombudsman estimated that close to 500 Colombian activists have been murdered since the beginning of 2016, a majority of them Indigenous human-rights defenders. In 2020, hostile actors killed more than 110 Indigenous activists, environmentalists, and journalists across the country.

Colombia is abundant with biodiversity, and forests cover nearly half of its land. This includes approximately 14,000,000 square miles of the Amazon rain forest. Much of this biodiverse area belongs to resource-rich Indigenous reserves. For many Indigenous groups, the concept of home extends beyond their immediate dwellings and to the plants and forests of these territories (or departments). These natural surroundings provide living spaces, sacred spaces, and spaces of healings. Rain forests benefit people outside these territories and cultures as well, producing the oxygen people breathe planet-wide. However, as a result of the areas' resources, both these habitats and their inhabitants are at risk.

In departments such as Cauca, Nariño, Chocó, and others, mining operations—legal and illegal— have encroached on the natural habitat. Indigenous groups in these areas include the Nasa, in Cauca; the Pastos, in Nariño; and the Emberá, in Chocó. Chocó has a substantial Afro-Colombian population as well. Throughout such departments, local peoples who oppose these land-grabbing and extraction efforts often meet with death threats or violence from the armed employees of mining and energy companies. Similar violence has resulted from the seizing of forest land for cattle rearing and from disputes over land on which people grow coca plants. The threat of armed groups is ongoing; according to the Environmental Justice Foundation, 2019 and 2020 were some of the deadliest recorded years for the defenders of these territories. Colombian human-rights activists allege that government authorities have failed to protect these territories and their peoples or to provide humanitarian aid. When mining or similar operations displace Indigenous peoples, safer conditions elsewhere may not be available. More than 40 percent of Colombia's total population lives in poverty, and the overcrowded urban housing depicted in *Amazona* is a reality for some of the displaced. But a return may not always be possible, as these operations can destroy the contested environments.

Indigenous peoples have experienced armed violence not just recently but throughout Colombia's history. For decades, the Colombian military and rebel group the Revolutionary Armed Forces of Colombia (FARC) were engaged in a civil war, putting people who belonged to neither party in the crossfire. This civil war ended in 2016, upon the signing of peace accords between the government

and FARC. But new patterns of violence erupted following the peace accords. Other armed groups moved to control the territories formerly occupied by FARC rebels, such as the coca-growing regions of the west and southwest. As a result, peoples of rural communities, especially activists and Indigenous leaders, remain at risk. Deforestation has also accelerated. In the years directly following the 2016 agreement, close to 1.2 million acres of the Colombian Amazon were destroyed.

In spite of these hardships, the Indigenous peoples of Colombia continue to show leadership and resilience. In October 2020, Indigenous leaders launched a gathering known as a minga in response to paramilitary killings in Indigenous communities, government neglect, and the abuses of government-aligned businesses. Derived from the Quechua term *minka*, a minga involves the widespread mobilization of peoples for the purpose of working toward the common good. In this case, it involved thousands of peoples from different Indigenous and Afro-Colombian groups, many of them from the southwestern part of the country.

Participants in the minga gathered first in the city of Cali and requested a dialogue with Colombian president Iván Duque. When Duque did not honor this request, the minga began a move to Colombia's capital city, Bogotá, traveling in a caravan miles long. The minga reached Bogotá on October 19, and on October 21, minga leaders declared their intent to stay in the capital, where they would take part in nationwide strikes against poverty and inequality. These strikes, promoted by a coalition of activists, students, teachers, doctors, and other Colombians, have advanced a protest against government policies—in particular, a change to taxation during the COVID-19 pandemic. Strikers and the Indigenous Minga have encountered violence both from government security forces and from armed civilians acting on police encouragement. Human-rights organizations have reported unwarranted detentions, sexual assaults, and disappearances. However, even under these threats, the national strikes and the Indigenous Minga continued into 2021, voicing demands for equality and a more just future.

SELECTED BIBLIOGRAPHY

Allen, Nicolas. "Colombians Don't Just Want a New Government—They Want an End to Neoliberalism: An Interview with Forrest Hylton." *Jacobin*, May 16, 2021. https://jacobinmag.com/2021/05/colombia -protests-strike-2021-duque-uribismo-neoliberalism-police.

Cultural Survival. "Cultural Survival Condemns the Massacre of Indigenous Leaders in Colombia." November 1, 2019. https://www.culturalsurvival.org/news/cultural-survival-condemns-massacre-indigenous-leaders-colombia.

Feng, Deon. "Risking Death to Defend Life in Colombia." Globe Post, December 4, 2020. https://theglobepost.com /2020/12/04/colombia-human-rights-defenders.

International Work Group for Indigenous Affairs. "Indigenous Peoples in Colombia." IWGIA. Accessed July 8, 2021. https://www.iwgia.org/en/colombia.html.

Mendoza, Diana. "The Indigenous World 2021: Colombia." IWGIA, March 18, 2021. https://www.iwgia.org/en /colombia/4212-iw-2021-colombia.html.

ProPacífico. "Pacific Region." Accessed July 8, 2021. https://propacifico.org/en/about-us/region-pacifico.

Trent, Steve. "As Indigenous Peoples Protest in Colombia, We Must Rally with Them." Environmental Justice Foundation, November 12, 2020. https://ejfoundation.org/news-media/as-indigenous-people-protest-in -colombia-we-must-rally-with-them.

ABOUT THE AUTHOR

Canizales is a Colombia-born author-illustrator living in Majorca, Spain.
His books have been published in Spanish, English, Basque, Chinese, French,
Greek, Italian, Korean, Macedonian, Polish, Portuguese, and Ukrainian.
Spanish honors for his art include the 2019 Cuatrogatos prize (shortlisted),
the 2018 Cuatrogatos prize, the 2018 Ciudad de Palma Comic Awards
(honorary mention), and the 2017 Divina Pastora social graphic novel award.
He also works as a professor of drawing at Universitat Oberta de Catalunya.